**KENTUCKY DEPARTMENT
FOR
LIBRARIES AND ARCHIVES
P. O. Box 537
Frankfort, Kentucky 40602-0537**

RUSSELL
AND
ELISA

By Johanna Hurwitz

Johanna Hurwitz
RUSSELL
AND
ELISA

Illustrated by Lillian Hoban

Morrow Junior Books
New York

Printed in the United States of America.
1 2 3 4 5 6 7 8 9 10

Library of Congress Cataloging-in-Publication Data
Hurwitz, Johanna.
Russell and Elisa / Johanna Hurwitz ; illustrated by Lillian
Hoban.
p.   cm.
Summary: Seven-year-old Russell and his three-year-old sister Elisa have adventures with friends and family in their apartment building.
ISBN 0-688-08792-2.—ISBN 0-688-08793-0 (lib. bdg.)
[1. Brothers and sisters—Fiction.]   I. Hoban, Lillian, ill.
II. Title.
PZ7.H9574Rs   1989   88-37578
[E]—dc19   CIP
                                                            AC

To the Great Neck Library
on its one-hundredth birthday,
and to all my friends there

Contents

The Package

Even though Elisa Michaels was not as big as her big brother, Russell, she was not as little as she used to be. It's true she didn't go to school like Russell, who was in second grade. And it's true she couldn't tell time or tie her own shoelaces. But she dressed herself these days—if somebody helped with the buttons.

1

After all, on her next birthday Elisa was going to be four, and four was much, much older than three.

In fact, Elisa was so big that, three mornings a week, she went to a play group. Six children met together in Mrs. Newman's apartment. They baked cookies and drew pictures and played games. It was fun going to the play group. It was almost like going to school. Russell said play group was not like school at all. Elisa knew he was wrong. *She* was right.

On days when Elisa didn't have play group, she helped her mother with her errands. When they went to the supermarket, she helped her decide what to cook for dinner.

"String beans or green peas?" asked Mrs. Michaels as they stood in the produce department.

"Peas," said Elisa.

"Hamburgers or lamb stew?" asked Mrs.

Michaels when they reached the meat counter.

"Hamburgers," said Elisa. She knew all the answers.

What Elisa liked most was helping her mother at the post office. Elisa loved the post office, where her mother went to buy stamps and from time to time send off packages. At home, Elisa watched when her mother wrote letters to her grandmother, who lived in California. Then her mother would put the letter into an envelope. Sometimes she would include a special drawing that Elisa made in the envelope, too. Next Mrs. Michaels wrote the address on the envelope. Then she gave Elisa a postage stamp, and Elisa licked it with her tongue and pasted it in the corner. Without a stamp on it, the mail carrier would not deliver the letter. So pasting on the stamp was very special and important.

"I went to the post office today," Elisa told Russell when he came home from school.

"So what," said Russell. He was already seven going on eight. His mother insisted that once upon a time he, too, had liked going to the post office. But Russell didn't believe her. She probably just said it to make Elisa feel better.

"I pasted the stamps on *five* letters," said Elisa.

"Big deal," he answered.

"One of the stamps was an airmail stamp, and the letter is going to fly on an airplane all the way to France."

"You don't even know where France is," said Russell. He said that even though he didn't know, either.

"It's far, far away," said Elisa. "That's why the letter is going on an airplane."

"So what."

It was hard to impress a brother who was so old, Elisa thought to herself sadly.

"I wish I would get a letter," Elisa told her mother every day when the mail was delivered to their apartment building.

"You will when you are older and write letters to other people," Mrs. Michaels promised.

Elisa stood watching as the mailman put the letters in the boxes of all the people who lived in their apartment building. Even though she couldn't read at all, she had learned which were the boxes of her friends. "Nora and Teddy are getting a lot of mail today," she remarked to her mother.

"Everyone is getting a lot of mail today," said Mrs. Michaels. "It's the start of a new month and we're all getting bills."

Elisa didn't know about bills. But she kept watching and hoping. One of these days there would be a letter for her.

"If you write a letter to Grandma, I'm sure she will write back to you," suggested Mrs. Michaels one rainy afternoon.

"Could I put it in an envelope all by itself?" asked Elisa. "An envelope that doesn't have a letter from you?"

"Sure," said her mother.

Elisa took a clean sheet of paper and made scribble-scrabble lines all over it. "Here," she said.

Mrs. Michaels shook her head. "Let me spell the words for you," she suggested. "Grandma will have trouble reading this." So, with her mother's help, Elisa carefully wrote out all the letters to make up a big letter. It read:

DEAR GRANDMA
ZEND ME
A LETTER.
LOVE ELIZA

It was very hard work writing so many ABC letters to make up a letter that you could mail. Elisa was quite tired by the time the letter was finished.

"Oh, dear, you forgot to write *please*," said Mrs. Michaels.

"So what," said Elisa, sounding a bit like Russell. She knew she couldn't write one more word to her grandmother.

"It's important to be polite," her mother reminded her. "But I think Grandma will be so happy to get a letter from you that she will understand that just this once you forgot."

"Will she really write a letter back to me?" asked Elisa as she licked the stamp to put on the envelope that her mother had addressed for her.

"I'm sure she will," said Mrs. Michaels.

Later, when the rain stopped, they walked to a mailbox that was a block away. Mrs. Michaels lifted Elisa up so she could open the box and let her letter drop inside. She listened and could hear it fall to the bottom of the huge red-white-and-blue mailbox. Now her letter was on its way to Grandma.

They stopped to buy some apples at the fruit store and then they went home.

"Open our mailbox," said Elisa as they entered the lobby of their apartment building. "Maybe Grandma answered my letter."

"We already had a mail delivery," said Mrs. Michaels. "Besides, Grandma hasn't received your letter yet. It will take a few days until she gets it, and at least a few more days until her answer comes for you."

Elisa was disappointed about that. But when Russell came home from school, she bragged to him all the same. "I wrote a letter to Grandma all by myself. And she is going to write a letter to me. My mail will come on an airplane."

"How do you know?" asked Russell.

"Mommy said it will come on an airplane because California is so far away from New York."

Russell shrugged his shoulders. He had made a date to play upstairs with his friend Teddy. Elisa's letter didn't seem very important to him.

The next day, Elisa couldn't wait for her play group to end. "Did my letter come?" she asked her mother when Mrs. Michaels came to take her home.

She asked the same question every day for a week—even on Sunday, when there was no mail delivery.

Elisa asked the same question every day for a second week. She continued pasting stamps for her mother and watching the mailman sort out his deliveries, but there was nothing for her. She would never, never get a letter, she decided. At least not until she was much more grown-up, perhaps nine or ten.

And then one day when she and her mother returned from some errands, Elisa could see that there was something in their mailbox.

"Look," she shouted to her mother. "Maybe that's my letter."

9

"The mailman already came today," said Mrs. Michaels. "Don't you remember when I got the mail at lunchtime?"

But there was no doubt about it, there was something inside their box. Mrs. Michaels put her bag of groceries on the floor and opened the little box. Inside was a small piece of yellow paper.

"It's not an envelope," Elisa said, sighing. "It's not my letter."

"No. It's a notice from the delivery truck. They tried to leave a package for us, and there was no one home to sign for it. We will have to go to the post office to pick it up."

"I don't want to," grumbled Elisa. "I'm tired."

She remembered that the last time a package arrived, it had contained a big cheese that someone had sent them as a gift. Cheese was a silly present. She didn't feel like walking all the way to the post office just to get another package of cheese.

"I have a surprise to show you. Look," said

her mother, holding out the yellow paper that had been in the mailbox. "It says that there is a package for E. Michaels. Do you know who that is?"

"No," said Elisa, shaking her head.

"E is for Elisa. No one else in this family has the initial E. That means that the package at the post office is for you."

Elisa jumped up. Suddenly she wasn't even the least bit tired at all. "Hurry, hurry," she said to her mother. "Maybe the post office will close."

First they had to go upstairs to their apartment and put the groceries away. "Hurry," Elisa kept saying. She couldn't wait to get her package.

Mrs. Michaels and Elisa went off to the post office. Mrs. Michaels handed the woman behind the window the yellow slip. The woman went away and returned with a big package. Mrs. Michaels wrote on the bottom of the slip, and the package was handed over.

"Shall we wait to get home to open this?"

11

asked Mrs. Michaels as she showed Elisa the letters of her name on the package.

"No," said Elisa, clutching her package. She smelled it suspiciously. It didn't smell like cheese. "I want to open it right here in the post office."

"All right," agreed her mother. She lifted Elisa up to the table at which people stood addressing their envelopes and pasting stamps on them.

Opening the package was even harder than buttoning her buttons in the morning, and so after a few moments, Mrs. Michaels helped. But it was Elisa herself who opened the box that was under the brown wrapping paper. It was not cheese at all. Inside the box there was a funny doll, different from any Elisa had ever seen before. There was a letter, too.

"I will read it to you," said Mrs. Michaels, taking the paper from Elisa. "It's from Grandma. She says: 'Dear Elisa. Here is a rag doll that I made for you. I had one just like it that my grandmother made for me when I was your age.

12

I hope you will like the one I've made for you. I decided not to wait until your birthday because sometimes it's fun to get a present on an ordinary day. Tell Russell I'm going to send him a present soon, too. Love, Grandma.' "

Elisa studied her new doll. Its hair was made of brown yarn. The eyes were sewn onto the face, and they didn't open and close like the eyes on dolls she had at home. The doll was wearing a blue jumper and a long-sleeved shirt that had tiny flowers on it. She didn't have any shoes, and her nose was just a couple of stitches sewn on her face. But she was soft to hug, and she smelled good, too.

"I love getting mail," said Elisa, smiling at her doll.

Later, when Russell saw it, he said, "That's a stupid doll. It doesn't do anything. It can't cry and it can't drink water and it doesn't speak." Those were the accomplishments of Elisa's other dolls. Russell was a little worried. He was afraid that the present his grandmother was going to send him would be another rag doll.

"It's a wonderful doll," said Elisa, "and she came to me especially in the mail."

"What are you going to name her?" asked Mr. Michaels as he admired the new toy.

"Airmail," said Elisa. "Because she came to me in the mail in an airplane."

"That's a stupid name for a stupid doll," said Russell.

Elisa shook her head. "It's a good name for a good doll," she insisted. And that night when she went to bed, she put the letter from her grandmother under her pillow. And she put Airmail into the bed with her, too. It was the perfect place for the perfect present that had arrived in the perfect way. Airmail.

The Haircut

Early in the afternoon one Thursday, Mrs. Michaels took Elisa to the local barbershop to get her bangs trimmed. The barber was the same man who always cut Russell's hair.

Elisa was a little bit afraid of sitting on the high infant seat the barber placed on top of the regular chair. But because she had brought Airmail along with her for company, she just hugged her doll tightly and didn't cry. She remembered from the last time that getting her hair cut didn't really hurt at all. It only tickled when the little bits of hair fell on her face. She held very still, just as the barber told her. She was so good that when he was finished, he gave her not one, not two, but three lollipops. Red, yellow, and orange.

"One is for you, one is for your brother, and the other is for your baby," the barber said.

"Airmail is not a baby," said Elisa. "She's a big girl like me." But nevertheless, she held tight to the extra lollipop. She knew Airmail was going to give it to her.

"I got my hair cut," Elisa shouted to Russell the minute he walked inside their apartment when school was over for the day.

"So what," said Russell.

"And I didn't cry," said Elisa proudly.

Russell was about to say "So what" for a

second time, but he suddenly thought of something. "Did you get a lollipop?"

"Yes, and I got one for you, too," said Elisa. She gave Russell the yellow one.

"Didn't you get a red one?" asked Russell. Red was his favorite color.

"Yes," said Elisa. "And I ate it all up."

"No fair," complained Russell.

"Yes it is," said Elisa. "It was my hair that got cut, so I ate the red one. You always pick the red one when you get your hair cut."

While they were discussing lollipops, the telephone rang. It was the mother of Annie Chu, a little girl who lived in the next building on their street. Annie and Elisa often played together. Mrs. Chu wanted to know if Annie could stay with Elisa for an hour while she went to the dentist for an emergency appointment.

Russell put the yellow lollipop in his mouth. He liked it much better when one of *his* friends came to play. Elisa's friends were all babies, and they had bad habits. There was Cissie, who always made a pig of herself. Tara was even worse. She once threw one of Russell's little cars into the toilet bowl. At least Annie Chu wouldn't do a thing like that.

"You go into your room and play now," said Mrs. Michaels when Annie arrived. "I have to finish chopping up these vegetables for the casserole for supper." The girls could hear the sound of the chopping machine as they joined Russell in the bedroom.

"Let's play barbershop," Elisa suggested to Annie. "We can give a haircut to Airmail."

"Can I be the barber?" asked Annie.

"You can be the barber, and then I'll be the barber. Airmail can get two pretend haircuts today," Elisa decided. She took the pillow off her bed and put it on a chair. Then she seated Airmail on top of the pillow. "Don't be afraid," she told her doll. "Haircuts don't hurt."

Elisa turned to Annie. "Airmail's bangs are

too long. They keep getting in her eyes." That was what Mrs. Michaels had said about Elisa's hair before she got it cut.

Next Elisa went to the bathroom and returned with a towel and a comb. She wrapped the towel around Airmail. "If Airmail is a good girl, she will get a lollipop when I finish." Elisa showed Russell and Annie the orange lollipop that was in her pocket, waiting to be eaten.

Russell watched as Elisa took her little scissors out of the box that held her crayons and other art supplies. She gave the scissors to Annie. "It's your turn first," she said.

Annie opened and closed the scissors, pretending to snip Airmail's yarn hair. Then she gave the scissors to Elisa, who also pretended to cut the doll's hair.

"Why don't you really cut some of her hair?" asked Russell. He was sitting on his bed and watching the girls. He kept his eye on Elisa's pocket with the lollipop inside. He hadn't known that Elisa had gotten an orange one.

Orange was his second favorite color, after red.

"We shouldn't really cut her hair," said Elisa, although she was tempted. "Just pretend."

"Sure you can," said Russell. He got his own scissors, which were a little sharper than Elisa's. He took a tiny snip of the brown yarn. Then he took another. Airmail was such a funny-looking doll that she probably would look better if he gave her a haircut, he thought.

Elisa and Annie laughed with delight. "Airmail is getting a real haircut, just like me," Elisa crowed.

Russell cut a few more little pieces of the doll's hair. "When I finish cutting Airmail's hair, I can cut your hair, too."

"I already had a haircut," said Elisa.

"Cut my hair," said Annie. "I haven't had a haircut in a long, long time."

Annie had very long hair. It was straight and dark and very shiny.

"I won't cut it all off," Russell promised. He was enjoying this game that Elisa had begun.

Elisa removed Airmail from the chair and gave the doll a big kiss for being such a grown-up girl and not crying at all during her haircut. Then Annie sat down on the chair.

"I'm ready," said Annie.

Russell took the towel and wrapped it around his sister's friend's neck. Then he took the comb and slowly moved it through Annie's hair. It was much more fun to play with real hair than with the yarn on the doll's head. He combed her hair gently, just as the barber always did.

At first he just pretended to snip at it. He held the scissors away from Annie's head, but his hand with the scissors kept coming closer and closer to her hair. "I'll just take the teeniest, tiniest little bit," he reassured Annie. He snipped, and a few small hairs landed on the towel. It was fun. Russell snipped again and then again.

23

"You're a good barber," said Elisa. She always loved to play with her big brother, but it wasn't often that they played a game that she thought up. Usually Russell made up the games, and the rules of the games, too.

"Hold still," said Russell to Annie, just as the barber always told him.

Annie held very still, and Russell cut some more of her hair. Cutting hair was much more fun than cutting paper, he thought. Annie's hair was still dark and shiny, but it no longer was as long as it had been before. Russell walked around the chair and cut on the other side of Annie's head to make it even all around.

"No more," said Annie. "That's enough."

"Wait," said Russell. "I just need to cut a little bit more from this side." He remembered how the barber always cut first from one side of his head and then the other, to be sure that both sides matched.

"No," said Annie, standing up. "I want to see how it looks."

The towel slipped off her shoulders, and the hair that Russell had cut off slid onto the floor.

"Now we have to sweep up the hair," Elisa said. "That's what they always do at the barbershop. I'll get the broom."

"Wait," called Russell. He had a feeling it would be better just to pick up Annie's hair with his fingers and flush it down the toilet without his mother knowing. She might not understand about playing barbershop.

He was right about that.

"Barbershop!" shouted Mrs. Michaels a few moments later. She had finished her work in the kitchen and was checking up on the children. "What do you mean, you've been playing barbershop?"

"We always play pretend games," said Elisa. She was proud of the game she had made up.

"This isn't pretend. This is real," said Mrs. Michaels. "Oh, Annie, honey. I'm so sorry. What will your mother say when she sees your beautiful hair is all gone?"

25

"Let me see," said Annie. She put her hand to her head. "It's not *all* gone. I still can feel hair," she insisted.

"Russell, I'm really ashamed of you," his mother said. "How could you do a thing like that?"

"Annie asked me to cut her hair," said Russell. He didn't understand why his mother was so angry about it. "We can clean up the floor. I didn't make such a big mess."

"You made a terrible mess of Annie's beautiful hair!" said Mrs. Michaels.

At that moment, the doorbell rang. It was Mrs. Chu, back from her dentist appointment.

Russell was afraid that now he would have two mothers scolding him. It didn't seem fair. Playing barber had been Elisa's idea. And cutting her hair had been Annie Chu's idea. He didn't think he should be blamed at all.

Luckily, Mrs. Chu didn't scold. "Hair always grows back," she said as she examined her daughter's haircut.

"I know, but Russell had no right to do such a terrible thing," said Mrs. Michaels.

"Boys will be boys," said Mrs. Chu.

Russell thought that was a silly thing to say. Of course boys will be boys, girls will be girls, dogs will be dogs, cows will be cows. But for some reason, his mother began to laugh, and then Mrs. Chu began to laugh. Elisa took Annie into the bathroom so she could look at herself in the mirror. Annie and Elisa were laughing, too. So Russell guessed he wouldn't be scolded anymore. He laughed with relief.

"Come, let's have a cup of tea," suggested Mrs. Michaels. So the two mothers went into the kitchen. Mrs. Michaels poured glasses of milk for the children, and she brought out a bag of gingerbread men cookies from the cupboard.

"Oh, yum!" exclaimed Russell. "I love to bite off the heads first."

"When it's cookies, you can cut off the head

or the feet," his mother said to Russell. "But you are never, never to cut off hair on Elisa or one of her friends or on yourself."

"When I'm a daddy, can't I shave?" asked Russell.

"Of course you can shave when you're grown," said his mother, laughing. "But until then, the only thing you're to cut is paper. Do you understand?"

Russell nodded his head.

Annie Chu had heard the story of the runaway gingerbread man in nursery school. But she had never seen a gingerbread man cookie. She and Elisa watched eagerly as Mrs. Michaels opened the bag of cookies.

"Oh, dear," said Mrs. Michaels as she tried to arrange the cookies on a plate. "The cookies are all broken." She pulled out pieces that were meant to be heads and bodies and legs.

"I want to see a whole gingerbread man," complained Annie.

28

"Me, too," cried Elisa. "These are no good."

"The cookie pieces taste delicious," said Mrs. Chu, eating one.

"They all get broken up into pieces once they're inside you, anyhow," said Mrs. Michaels.

But it was Russell who had the best answer of all. "The gingerbread men were fighting in the bag," he said. "That's why they are all broken."

"Fighting?" said Elisa. "Why were they fighting?"

"It's bad to fight," said Annie.

"Yes, it is," agreed both mothers.

"Fighting is much worse than cutting hair," said Russell.

Everyone agreed that he was right about that. The mothers drank their tea, and the children drank their milk, and they all ate the cookie pieces of the naughty gingerbread men who had fought themselves into bits.

When it was time for Annie to go home,

Elisa reached into her pocket. "This is for you," she said to Annie. She gave her friend the orange lollipop. "I always get a lollipop when I get my hair cut."

Annie smiled and accepted her gift.

And Russell knew better than to complain.

A Bad Dream

All day Saturday, Mr. and Mrs. Michaels were very busy. They were going to have company that evening. When Elisa asked her mother to cut out some paper dolls, she said, "I can't now, honey. I have to cut up the chicken for dinner."

When Russell asked his father to take him to

Woolworth's so he could look at the little cars on sale, Mr. Michaels replied, "I won't have time to take you there today. There are too many things that I have to get done around the house."

Just because their parents were having company, there was no time for anything else. Mr. and Mrs. Michaels were busy all day long. Mr. Michaels vacuumed the living room and dusted in all the corners.

Mrs. Michaels was cooking chicken for the guests, but she was fixing it in a different way than she did when it was just for the family. Elisa watched as her mother chopped up mushrooms and onions. She poured tomato sauce and wine into the pot with the cut-up chicken pieces. Elisa was glad she wouldn't have to eat that mishmash of food.

But then Mr. Michaels made a huge lime pie for dessert. He beat egg whites and squeezed limes and added sugar. That looked much more delicious than the chicken. Elisa and Russell scraped out the bowl to check it out. "You could make that kind of pie for us," said Elisa.

When Elisa and Russell and their parents ate dinner, they always sat around the kitchen table. But today, Mrs. Michaels set the table in the dining area. First she put the extra boards in the table to make it larger. Then she put a huge and beautiful cloth over the table. The cloth was so big that it hung down over the sides of the table and reached almost to the floor.

Elisa crawled under the table to see what it was like underneath. It was just like being inside a cave or a tent. A little light came through the cloth so she could look around, but no one could see her. It was a wonderful, cozy place to play. Elisa wished her mother would leave the cloth on the table every day so she could play under the table. For the rest of the afternoon, while Russell visited at his friend Jeremy's house, Elisa played quietly under the dining-room table. She took Airmail under the table with her. It was fun pretending to be inside a secret house all their own.

Mr. Michaels took Elisa with him when he went to pick up Russell at Jeremy's. Then, as a special treat, he took the two children to have pizza for their supper.

"Aren't you going to eat any pizza, Daddy?" Russell asked as he took a big bite from his slice.

"No. I'll be eating later with the company," he said. But he did eat the crusts that Elisa left. And he finished her orange drink, too.

"Why don't you have pizza for your company?" asked Russell. "That's what I would like to eat if I was company at someone's house."

"It's better than yucky chicken with mushrooms," said Elisa.

"Pizza is good," agreed their father. "But grown-ups like yucky chicken even better."

34

"I won't when I grow up," said Russell with certainty.

"Me, either," said Elisa.

When they got back to the apartment, Mrs. Michaels was dressed in a fancy long skirt and a blouse. The table was set with plates and wineglasses and even candles. It looked as if there was going to be a party.

"Is it a birthday?" asked Elisa.

"No, just a dinner party," her mother said, laughing. Mrs. Michaels helped Elisa get washed up and into her pajamas. Russell was big enough so that he didn't need any assistance at all.

Even though it wasn't a birthday, the guests brought presents. Russell and Elisa watched eagerly as their mother opened the wrapping paper on the packages. One was a bottle of wine. The second package was a bottle of wine, too. The third package was a box of colored soaps. Grown-up parties were not nearly as nice as parties for children, Elisa decided. She didn't like what they ate, and she didn't like their presents, either.

All of the grown-ups smiled at Russell and Elisa and told them how big they had grown since they had seen them last. Elisa couldn't remember ever seeing these people before.

"Now that you've met everyone, it's time for you both to get into bed," their father said.

"Already?" complained Russell.

"Already," he repeated. "If you're good, I'll save a piece of the lime pie for each of you for tomorrow."

"Yummy," said Elisa as she climbed into bed.

Mr. Michaels kissed the children good night. Then he turned off the light in their bedroom and closed the door.

Elisa snuggled under her covers and smiled into the dark. She was remembering the limey taste that she had scraped from the sides of the mixing bowl earlier that day. Tomorrow she would have a whole piece of pie to herself. She felt in her bed for Airmail. She always slept with her doll, but tonight she couldn't find her. She felt all over the top of her covers and then underneath them, but she couldn't find Airmail. She sat up in bed, wondering where her doll could be. Then she remembered. Airmail was underneath the dining-room table where they had played together during the afternoon.

Elisa wanted Airmail, but she didn't want to get out of bed and go into the room with all that company. So she lay back in her bed again and thought she would wait until all the guests went home. After they left, she would get her doll. It was hard to lie still and wait so long. She tried to remember how she fell asleep in the days before she had her soft rag doll for company. She couldn't remember. After turning over and over, she decided to go and get Airmail, after all.

Elisa got out of bed.

"Where are you going?" asked Russell, who was half asleep.

"I have to get Airmail," said Elisa.

"No you don't," he said.

"I can't sleep without her," said Elisa, opening the door to their bedroom.

"Mommy and Daddy will be angry if you bother them now," her brother warned.

"No they won't," said Elisa. "I'm coming right back."

Elisa tiptoed out into the hallway. The grown-ups were still sitting in the living room and talking together. No one even noticed Elisa as she went into the dining area. She ducked under the table and looked around. Sure enough, there was Airmail, lying on the floor, right where she had left her when she went out to have supper.

Elisa picked up her favorite doll and gave her a hug.

Just then, she heard the grown-ups coming toward the dining area. Chairs were pulled out as people took their places around the table. Elisa sat on the floor underneath and looked at all the legs and feet under the table. It was funny to see so many different kinds of shoes. Some had laces and some didn't. Elisa recognized her mother's shoes, each with a hole in front and a big toe sticking out.

Elisa knew she should get out from under the table. But suddenly, she felt shy about crawling out through all those feet. She decided that Russell was right. Her parents would be angry with her for getting out of bed. She thought she would wait until everyone was busy eating. Maybe she could sneak out without anyone noticing her.

She listened to the mumble of voices and the clatter of the dishes. She could hear her mother speaking, and other people answering. She heard the forks and knives on the plates. She heard laughing as someone said something funny. Elisa lay down on the floor with her arms around Airmail. It was strange to be so

close to so many people when they didn't even know she was there.

Suddenly, it was quiet. There wasn't a sound at all. Elisa sat up in the dark and felt for Air- mail. She picked up her doll and looked around. She couldn't see anything. She couldn't feel her pillow or her blanket. She thought they might have fallen on the floor, but she couldn't feel the sides of her bed, so she couldn't lean over and reach down to the floor. It was very scary. How could her bed and her blanket and her pillow all disappear in the night?

For a moment, Elisa sat holding Airmail tight and trying hard not to cry. But even with her soft doll for comfort, she could not hold back her sobs. Elisa began to howl.

After a few minutes, she heard faraway sounds. "I'll go to her," she thought she heard her father say. "She must be having a bad dream."

Elisa sniffed back her tears. Of course, she

41

thought, I'm having a bad dream. She sat waiting for her father to come and wake her up so she could stop dreaming. She heard the door to her bedroom open and she waited. But still her father didn't come.

"She's not there!" Mr. Michaels said to his wife.

"What do you mean, she's not there?" asked Mrs. Michaels anxiously. "Of course she's there."

Elisa listened as her mother and father talked together in the dark. Lights were turned on, but she still couldn't see very well.

"I am here," Elisa called to them. "Come and wake me up. I don't like my dream. It's scaring me."

"I hear her voice," cried Mrs. Michaels. "Listen."

"Elisa, where are you?" called her father.

"I'm in my bed," she cried. "I woke up, but I'm still having a bad dream."

More lights went on. Suddenly, it was very

bright and arms were scooping Elisa up. "For heaven's sake! What are you doing here?" exclaimed Mr. Michaels.

"Daddy!" Elisa sobbed. "I was having a bad dream."

"I was having a bad dream, too," said her father. "And so was your mother."

They took Elisa into the kitchen. Mrs. Michaels washed her daughter's face with a damp paper towel. She gave her a drink of water. "How in the world did you get under the dining table?" she asked.

Elisa tried to remember. Finally, she said, "I went to get Airmail." She looked around. "Where is Airmail?"

Mr. Michaels went out to the dining area and brought the doll from under the table.

"Are you ready to go back to sleep in your bed now?" asked Mrs. Michaels.

Elisa nodded.

Her father carried her all the way to the bedroom, just as he had when she was a little baby. He placed her in her bed and covered her up with her blanket. Then her mother put Airmail into bed beside her.

"Where's Russell?" asked Elisa.

"He's fast asleep in his bed, where he is supposed to be," Mrs. Michaels said. "I can't believe you were under the table all that time."

"I was," said Elisa. "It was fun at first. But it's not as nice as being in my bed."

"I should say not," agreed her mother, as first she, and then Mr. Michaels, leaned down and kissed Elisa. "Now go back to sleep," whispered Mrs. Michaels.

"I will," said Elisa. And she did.

A Night
Away from Home

One Friday afternoon, Russell got a telephone call. It was from his friend Teddy Resnick, who lived upstairs on the seventh floor of their apartment building.

"Nora has a sleep-over date at her friend Sharon's house," Teddy said. "So my mother told me I could invite you to sleep at our house. Okay?"

"A sleep-over date?" shouted Russell into the telephone receiver. Even though he was getting to be so grown-up these days, he had never had a sleep-over date with any of his friends. But he had heard Teddy and his sister Nora talk about sleep-over dates many times.

"Ask your mother if it's okay," said Teddy. "I hope she says yes, because we can have a lot of fun. You can sleep in Nora's bed."

Russell dropped the telephone receiver with a bang and ran to ask his mother for permission.

"I never ever had a sleep-over date," he pleaded. "Please say yes."

"Yes, you did," his mother said, laughing. "When I went to the hospital when Elisa was born in the middle of the night, your father took you upstairs to the Resnicks' to sleep."

"It doesn't count if I don't remember," said Russell. "Say yes, please. Pretty please with sugar on top."

"Of course you can," said his mother. "And

46

you can even wear those new pajamas that Grandma just sent you."

"Yippee," Russell sang out as he ran to the telephone to tell Teddy the good news.

"Can you come and have supper with me, too?" asked Teddy.

Russell had to drop the phone a second time to find out the answer to that question. Luckily, that answer was yes also. He felt so grown-up and so happy. It was too bad that this was a night when his mother was roasting a chicken. The whole apartment smelled good, and he had already begun to get hungry for it. Still, it was worth missing one of his favorite meals to have his first sleep-over date.

Mrs. Michaels gave Russell a shopping bag. "You can put your things in here," she said. "You'll need clean underwear for tomorrow and a clean T-shirt and your toothbrush. Here are your new pajamas. And don't forget your slippers."

Russell was especially proud of his new pajamas from his grandmother because they

looked like a baseball uniform. He had been
watching games on TV with his father lately
and learning all about baseball.

Elisa stood watching as Russell put a pair of
blue socks and his blue-and-white-striped T-
shirt into the shopping bag. "I wish I had a
sleep-over date, too," she said.

"You're too little," Russell pointed out.

"No I'm not," she said, pouting.

"I have a great idea," said Mrs. Michaels.
"Since Russell won't be here tonight, you can
have a sleep-over date in his bed. How would
you like that?"

"Yes, yes," agreed Elisa, jumping up and
down with pleasure. "Airmail and I never
slept in Russell's bed."

"I don't want anyone sleeping in my bed,"
complained Russell. "Elisa can't. She has her
own bed. She can't sleep in mine."

"Of course she has her own bed, and so do
you," said his mother. "But since you are
borrowing Nora's bed tonight, Elisa can borrow yours.

"Everyone is having a sleep-over date in another bed. And Elisa can sleep in your bed for one night. She won't hurt it. She's a big girl now and keeps dry all night long."

"Oh, all right," agreed Russell grudgingly. "Elisa can sleep in my bed. But not Airmail. I don't want any stupid dolls in my bed."

"Airmail is not stupid," said Elisa.

"Yes, she is," said Russell.

"Stop!" said Mrs. Michaels. "Russell. Do you want to sleep upstairs with Teddy and let Elisa and Airmail borrow your bed? It's up to you, but you can't do one without the other."

Russell looked at the shopping bag with his clothes. His new pajamas were resting on the top. It would be so much fun to wear them upstairs at Teddy's apartment that he decided he didn't care about Elisa and Airmail.

"Okay," said Russell. "They can sleep in my bed."

"Good," said Mrs. Michaels.

"Goody," shouted Elisa.

"Good," said Teddy when Russell arrived

49

upstairs at his apartment a little later. "You got here just in time to watch TV before supper."

When the boys sat down to supper, Russell was surprised to see that Mrs. Resnick was serving roast chicken for supper, too.

"That's just what my mommy was cooking," he crowed with delight.

"Chicken was on sale in the supermarket this week," said Mrs. Resnick. "I bet most of the people in this building, and up and down the street, too, are eating chicken tonight."

Russell was amazed at the thought of all those chicken dinners. In addition to chicken, the Resnicks also had rice and carrots. There were applesauce and cookies for dessert.

After supper, the boys took a shower together. At home, Russell always took a bath. A shower was extra fun, with the water splashing down on his head and Teddy laughing and standing beside him. After the shower, Russell dried himself and put on his brand-new pajamas and his old slippers.

They played with Teddy's toy trains, and when they got tired of that, they sat on Nora's bed and played a game of cards. After a while, Teddy's mother came into the room. "All right, fellows. It's time for bed."

"We are in bed," said Teddy.

"That's not quite what I mean, and you know it," said Mrs. Resnick, smiling.

They put the cards away, and Russell climbed into Nora's bed. Teddy got into his own bed across the room.

"Good night," said Mrs. Resnick. She bent down and kissed Teddy on the forehead. Then she came over and gave Russell a kiss, too. "Good night, sleep tight, don't let the bedbugs bite," she said as she turned off the light switch.

"Do you have bugs in your beds?" Russell asked anxiously.

"That's just a joke," said Teddy. "She says it every night."

Russell thought it was a strange thing to say.

His mother never said anything like that. Russell began to feel something scratchy on the back of his neck. He wondered if it was a bug. He sat up in the dark and rubbed his neck. If he had worn his old pajamas with feet, he would have been more protected from the bugs.

Russell got out of bed.

"Where are you going?" asked Teddy. "Do you have to go to the bathroom?"

"I have to go downstairs and get my other pajamas," said Russell. He felt along the floor next to the bed for his slippers. "I'll be right back," he told his friend.

Russell went out into the living room. Teddy's parents were listening to music and reading. "Is something wrong?" asked Mr. Resnick.

"I just have to go downstairs for a minute," Russell explained.

"I'll call your parents and tell them that you are on the way," said Teddy's father.

Russell went out into the hall and pushed the elevator button. He had never been in the elevator in his pajamas before. When he got to the second floor, his mother was standing at the open door to their apartment, waiting for him. "What is the problem?" she asked.

"These new pajamas are itchy," Russell complained, rubbing his neck. He didn't want to tell his mother about the bugs.

Mrs. Michaels felt inside the neck of Russell's new pajamas. She tore out the label that was there. "I bet this was bothering you," she said. "You'll be fine now."

The pajamas did feel much better now that the label had been removed. "You didn't give me a good-night kiss," he remembered.

"You're right," his mother agreed. She bent down and gave him a kiss.

"Good night," said Russell. "I'll see you in the morning." He went back into the elevator, and in another minute he was back at Teddy's apartment.

Teddy was still awake in bed. "I'm glad you came back," he said. "I thought maybe you were going to sleep in your own house."

"Oh, no," said Russell. "I couldn't do that. This is my sleep-over date."

He lay down again. His neck didn't itch anymore. There didn't seem to be any bugs in the bed, either. He lay back and tried to sleep. The only problem was that the pillow didn't feel the way his pillow did in his bed. He punched the pillow with his fists, trying to make it feel different. But it didn't work. If only he had his own pillow from his own bed, he knew he would be asleep in a second.

Russell got out of bed again.

"Where are you going?" asked Teddy.

"I need to get something else," Russell said.

"Oh," said Teddy. "Don't forget to come back."

"I won't," promised Russell. He put on his slippers in the dark and made his way out of the room again.

"I have to get something else," he told Teddy's parents.

"I'll call your parents," Mrs. Resnick said, and she smiled.

This time, Russell's father was waiting at the door. "What is it now?" he asked. "Did you change your mind about sleeping over?"

"No. But I can't sleep without my own pillow," said Russell.

"Come inside, then," said his father. Russell followed his father into his own bedroom. Mr. Michaels took the pillow from Elisa's empty bed, and very gently, so as not to wake Elisa, who was sleeping soundly in Russell's bed, he lifted his daughter's head. He substituted one pillow for the other. Elisa did not wake up, which was a good thing.

"Do you need anything else?" he asked.

"Could I have a drink of water?"

"Sure."

So Russell had a small drink of water, even though they had water upstairs at Teddy's apartment, too. Then he took his own pillow and went up on the elevator and back to Teddy's apartment.

Russell put Nora's pillow down on the floor and put his own pillow on the bed. It felt soft

and comfortable, just as it did in his own bed. "Teddy," he whispered into the dark. But Teddy didn't answer. He must have fallen asleep already. Russell lay back on his pillow and tried to fall asleep, too. His hand rubbed against the blanket. It didn't feel soft and cozy the way his blanket did on his own bed at home. He wished he had thought to take his blanket when he took his pillow. He tried to fall asleep, but without his own cozy blanket, it was impossible.

Russell got out of bed again. In the dark, he felt around for his slippers. They were underneath Nora's pillow, but he found them. He walked out to the living room. "I need one more thing," he explained.

"Are you sure? Maybe you don't really need it," said Teddy's mother.

"I really need it," he said. "But this is the last thing."

"All right," said Mrs. Resnick, sighing. "I'll call downstairs and tell them you're on your way."

Russell got out of the elevator to find his mother waiting for him once again. "I think you are having a sleep-over date inside the elevator tonight," said his mother.

"No I'm not," said Russell. "But I need to get my own blanket. I don't like Nora's blanket."

They tiptoed again into the room where Elisa was sleeping. "Here," said his mother, "hold this a moment." She picked up Airmail, who was lying on top of the covers, and handed the doll to Russell. Then, gently, so as not to disturb Elisa, she removed the blanket and gave that to Russell, too. She took the blanket from Elisa's bed and put it over her daughter. Then she put Airmail back on the bed next to Elisa.

"That blanket is heavy to carry," said Mrs. Michaels. "Can you manage it?"

"Sure," said Russell. "I'm very grown-up, don't forget."

"All right," said his mother. "But in a little while, your father and I are going to bed. So if you come downstairs one more time, you will have to stay down. And if you stay downstairs,

58

you will sleep in Elisa's bed, because I am not going to move her from your bed the way we moved the pillow and the blanket. Do you understand?"

"Yes," said Russell. He certainly did not want to sleep in Elisa's bed.

His mother took his blanket from him and folded it up neatly so it was easier to carry. Then she bent down and kissed him one more time. "Good night," said his mother. "I'll see you in the morning."

"Good night," said Russell. He went into the elevator and back up to the seventh floor. Mrs. Resnick was waiting at the door.

"You are sure you have everything now?" she asked.

"Oh, yes," said Russell, nodding his head in agreement.

"You don't sleep with a teddy bear, do you? Because if you do, you should get it right now."

"I don't sleep with a teddy bear. I'm not a baby," said Russell. "Elisa sleeps with her silly doll Airmail, but I don't need anything special like that to go to sleep."

"Good," said Mrs. Resnick.

Russell pulled Nora's blanket off the bed and threw it on the floor. Then he arranged his own blanket. He took off his slippers and got into the bed. His new pajamas didn't scratch him, and his pillow was comfortable under his head. His blanket felt soft and cozy, just as it did at home. Having a sleep-over date was fun. It was almost like being at home, he thought as he began to fall asleep. He hoped Teddy would invite him to sleep over often, now that he was so grown-up.

Take Me Out
to the Ball Game

It seemed to Russell that he had been wanting to go to a real baseball game for a hundred years.

"It can't be a hundred years," said his father. "You're only seven years old."

Still, no matter what his father said, he'd been waiting a very long time. Now at last, he was finally going to the stadium to see a real baseball game. He was very excited, but he was also a little bit angry because Elisa was coming, too.

"It isn't fair," said Russell. "Elisa didn't have to wait until she was seven, and besides, she doesn't even understand anything about baseball."

"We're a family and we do things together," his mother reminded him. And so one Saturday morning the whole Michaels family set off for a baseball game together. But as if it weren't bad enough that Elisa was coming, she brought Airmail along, too.

"It's stupid to bring a doll to a baseball game," Russell grumbled. He was wearing a baseball cap and trying to appear very grown-up. It seemed babyish to sit next to Elisa on the subway while she held tightly to her rag doll.

"Airmail wants to see the baseball game, too," said Elisa.

Russell turned his head and pretended that he wasn't related to Elisa.

They took two subway trains and then they walked. Lots of people were walking in the same direction. You could tell that they were going to the baseball game, too. They went through a turnstile and up two huge escalators and up some steps until they finally came to their seats. The seats were very high up, and when Russell looked down, the baseball players looked very small. They were much smaller than they looked when Russell watched a baseball game with his father on TV.

"Did the game start already?" asked Russell. There was so much activity on the field that he wasn't sure what was happening.

"No. The players are just warming up," said Mr. Michaels.

After a while, a voice came over the loudspeaker and announced the names of all the men who would be playing that day.

Russell tried to remember the names, but there were too many. He looked over at Elisa and saw that she was whispering to Airmail.

"I'm telling Airmail all about baseball," said Elisa.

"You don't even know anything about baseball," said Russell. But there were too many things happening in the stadium for him to have time to pay attention to Elisa. Men were walking up and down the aisles selling all sorts of things: hot dogs, soda, ice cream, peanuts, yearbooks, pretzels.

They shouted out to the people, "Hot dogs. Get your hot dogs here!"

Mr. Michaels waved his arm, and the man stopped and made a sale. Russell bit into his hot dog with pleasure. A hot dog tasted even better at a baseball game than it did at home.

Everyone stood when they played "The Star-Spangled Banner." Russell knew all the

words because they sang the same song at his school.

At last the baseball game began!

Someone hit the ball, and Elisa gave a loud cheer. Russell was just about to cheer, too, when his father said, "That was a hit for the other team. We only cheer when our team hits the ball." So Russell was glad he hadn't cheered, after all. There were so many baseball players on the field and they were so small that it was hard to be sure what was happening all the time.

After a while, the men in the field went running toward the dugout, and the other men took their places at all the bases and in the outfield. Russell understood that. He looked over at Elisa to see if she understood, too.

"Is the game over?" asked Elisa.

"A baseball game is divided into nine innings," Mr. Michaels explained. "Each team has a turn hitting the ball during each inning.

66

This is still the first inning. We have a long way to go before the game is over."

"Good," said Elisa. "Airmail and I don't want to go home. We like baseball."

How could a doll like baseball? Russell wondered. Elisa sure was dumb.

Mr. Michaels bought cups of soda for everyone because they were thirsty from their hot dogs.

"Is the game over now?" asked Elisa as the men ran in from the field again.

"No. This is just the top of the second inning," said her father. "A baseball game has nine innings," he reminded her.

"I know that," said Elisa. "But Airmail gets confused about it."

Russell watched as the man at the plate hit the ball so high that it flew into the seats at the other end of the stadium.

"Oh, no," groaned Mr. Michaels, and the people sitting around them groaned also. "A home run."

"Is that bad?" asked Elisa.

"It's bad when it's not your team that gets it," her father said.

Even Russell knew that. Boy, was Elisa dumb.

Other men hit the ball, too. But they were always on the wrong team. Some of the fans in the stadium began to chant, "We want a hit." Soon, all around them, people were chanting the same words. When his father began to clap his hands and say the words, too, then Russell knew it was all right for him to do it also.

Someone from their team hit the ball and Russell cheered. But his father said the ball had gone foul and so it wouldn't count.

Some people got up to buy more hot dogs or to go to the rest rooms.

"Is it over?" asked Elisa.

"It's almost over," her father said, and sighed. "We're losing five to nothing, and it's the sixth inning."

68

Russell was good in arithmetic at school, so he knew there were three more innings to go. He also could figure out that his team would need at least six runs if they were going to win. It didn't seem fair. Here he was at his very first real baseball game and his team was losing.

"Can I have an ice cream?" he asked as he saw the man who was selling it approach them.

Mr. Michaels bought ice cream for both Russell and Elisa.

After a short while, all the people around them stood up. "It's the seventh-inning stretch," said Mrs. Michaels. "We should all stand up and stretch our legs. Does anyone need to use the rest room?"

No one did, so Russell and his parents and Elisa and Airmail all stood and stretched their legs. When they sat down, the game continued. "This is ridiculous," said a man sitting next to Elisa. He got out of his seat, saying, "I've seen enough. I'm going home."

"But the game isn't over," Elisa said to him.

"It's over for me," the man said.

Some other people also left their seats.

Russell stood, too. He didn't want to watch anymore if his team wasn't going to win the game. "Let's go home," he said.

"A baseball game has nine innings," shouted Elisa. "I don't want to go home yet. It's not over."

"That's right, kid," said a man sitting behind them. "It's not over till it's over."

"Oh, it's over all right," said someone else.

Mr. and Mrs. Michaels remained seated, so Russell sat down, too, but he didn't feel like watching. "Why did we pick such a bad game?" he asked, sulking.

"You never know how a game is going to turn out," Mr. Michaels said. "The strongest teams have bad days, and the worst teams can surprise you. If you knew your team was going to win before the game even started, it wouldn't be any fun to watch."

"Airmail and I don't care who wins the game," Elisa announced proudly.

That showed how little she knew about baseball, Russell thought. Still, his father had a point. If they knew their team would win, it wouldn't be as exciting.

Just then the pitcher lost control of the ball and accidentally hit the batter. That meant that the batter for Russell's team could walk to first base. The next hitter hit a ground ball between the legs of the pitcher. By the time the shortstop got the ball, there was a man on both first and second.

"We want a hit," shouted Mr. Michaels, and the remaining fans all began to chant the words, too. "We want a hit."

Russell began to shout the words, too. Maybe, just maybe, his team would surprise everyone and win the game after all.

The next hitter slammed the ball so hard with the bat that the bat cracked in two. Russell could actually see the two pieces lying on the ground. By the time he shifted his eyes to see where the ball was, the man on second had scored, and the man on first had reached third base.

"Was that a home run?" asked Elisa.

"That was a sacrifice fly," said her father. "But it's the beginning of a rally. We've finally scored a run, and we have a man on third with only one out."

Russell liked the way his father said that—as if *they* had done the hitting and the running instead of just sitting in the stands and watching the game.

Next there were back-to-back home runs.

"Now, that's more like it," shouted the man who was sitting behind them. "I told you it's not over till it's over."

"And there's still only one out," shouted Mr. Michaels. He turned to Russell and rubbed his hand in Russell's hair. "You picked a pretty good game for your first one," he said.

By the end of the inning, the score was tied. And by the end of the game, Russell's team had won.

"I guess you're glad your little girl insisted that you stay till the end," said the man who had been sitting behind them.

"You said it," said Russell's father. "This was one terrific game!"

Russell felt so good about his team winning that he sat next to Elisa on the subway and forgot to be embarrassed about Airmail. Airmail had a smudge of mustard on her face, just like Elisa.

When they got home, Eugene Spencer, who was one of their neighbors and who was eleven years old, was standing in the lobby, waiting for the elevator.

"We went to the baseball game today," announced Russell proudly. "It was super, and our team won."

"Did Elisa go, too?" asked Eugene Spencer, looking at the little girl. "She's too little. I bet she doesn't understand the first thing about baseball."

"I do too," said Elisa.

"She's learned the important things," said Russell, defending his sister. "She knows that a baseball game has nine innings and it's not over till it's over."

"Oh, pooh," said Eugene Spencer. "There's loads more to baseball than that."

"I know," said Russell, who had learned a lot about baseball that day, too. "But those are the most important things of all."

Lost

Almost every week, Mrs. Michaels took Russell and Elisa to the public library. Russell had his own card and picked out books that he could read by himself. Elisa was going to get a card one day soon, too. In the meantime, she used her mother's card. Every week she picked out books with bright-colored pictures

75

and funny stories that her parents read to her.

"Why do you bring that stupid doll with you all the time?" Russell grumbled when they set out for the library one Friday afternoon. Wherever Elisa went these days, she took Airmail. "You look silly."

"No I don't," said Elisa. "I need Airmail."

In the children's room of the library, there were many other boys and girls picking out books, too. Russell returned the books that he had borrowed the week before and then went right over to the shelves of "easy readers." He sat on the floor and made a pile of the books that he would take home. There was a new book about Frog and Toad that he had never read, and he found another book about Amelia Bedelia, too.

Elisa and their mother looked through the picture books. Elisa always wanted to take home books that they had read before. "Airmail likes that one," she would say when Mrs. Michaels protested that they had borrowed the same book four times in the past few months. Before she had received Airmail, Elisa used to say that her friend KiKi liked the books. Nowadays, she didn't talk much about the imaginary KiKi.

Today their mother convinced Elisa to take home three books that she had never borrowed before, in addition to three old favorites. Mrs. Michaels checked out the six books for Elisa, and Russell checked out the four books he had selected for himself.

"We'll just stop for a loaf of bread at the bakery," Mrs. Michaels said as they started for home.

Russell noticed that Elisa was holding two of her library books. He didn't see Airmail. He was about to mention that the doll was missing when he thought better of it. Why should he tell Elisa about the doll? If she didn't look after her own stupid toy, it meant that the doll wasn't so important to her after all. He liked walking along with his mother and his sister without the doll.

At the bakery, the woman behind the

counter gave both Russell and Elisa a cookie. And instead of saying that they had to wait until after supper to eat them, Mrs. Michaels gave the children permission to have them immediately. So what with nibbling on their cookies and the absence of the silly doll, Russell found that the trip home from the library was much more pleasant than the trip there.

It was when they got home that things became terrible.

"Where is Airmail?" Elisa screeched as they entered the elevator. She had suddenly noticed that she wasn't holding her doll.

Mrs. Michaels was carrying four library books and the paper bag with the bread inside it. Russell was carrying his four library books and Elisa had two library books. No one had Airmail.

"Did you put the doll down at the bakery?" asked her mother. "Come, we can walk back to the bakery and see if Airmail is there."

"Do we have to walk back there?" complained Russell. He knew the doll wasn't at the bakery.

"It won't take us long," said Mrs. Michaels.

Russell thought that perhaps the woman behind the counter would give him another cookie, and so he followed along with his mother and his sister. He didn't mention that he knew Airmail wasn't at the bakery.

There were many more people in the bakery now than there had been just fifteen minutes earlier. People on their way home from work were busy buying fresh bread and desserts for their families.

There was no sign of Airmail in the shop.

"Airmail," Elisa said, sobbing. "I want Airmail."

The woman behind the counter said she hadn't seen Airmail. She didn't offer them any more cookies, either, even though Elisa was crying so hard.

"You better check with the post office," said

79

an elderly man who didn't understand what she was crying about.

"The only other place that Airmail can be is at the library," said Mrs. Michaels. "Unless you dropped her along the way."

"Airmail. I want Airmail," Elisa cried.

"Come, we will retrace our steps," said Mrs. Michaels. It was getting dark now, but their mother insisted that they walk slowly along the same route that they had traveled before.

"My books are too heavy," Russell complained. He was beginning to feel sorry that he hadn't mentioned the doll when they left the library. He didn't know they would have to walk so much. And it was even worse to walk in the street with his sister screaming and crying than it was to walk with her holding her old rag doll.

By the time they reached the library, it was after five-thirty P.M. The door was shut tight, and all the lights were off because the library was closed.

"Airmail. I want Airmail," Elisa cried.

Mrs. Michaels put the bag with the bread and the library books that she had been holding down on the step and picked up Elisa. "We will come to the library first thing tomorrow morning," she said as she kissed her daughter. "We will ask if anyone saw Airmail."

Elisa kept sobbing. "I want Airmail *now*."

Russell kicked and banged on the library door. He hoped someone was inside and would open it. Unfortunately, no one responded to his banging.

They made their way home again, with Elisa sobbing all the way. As they entered the lobby for the second time, they saw Nora and Teddy and their mother.

"What's the matter, Elisa?" asked Nora.

"Airmail. I want Airmail," the little girl said again and again, still sobbing.

Nora knew Elisa meant her doll. "Where is Airmail?" she asked. "Is she upstairs in your house?"

"We seem to have left Airmail in the

library," Mrs. Michaels explained. "We're going to go back and look for her first thing in the morning."

"You could borrow one of my dolls for tonight," Nora offered Elisa. "Remember all my dolls that you like to play with when you come to my apartment?"

It was true that Nora had a big collection of dolls that she hardly ever played with anymore. Russell saw them whenever he was in their apartment.

"Hey, Elisa," he said. "You could take Nora's doll that talks. The one that says, 'Mommy, Mommy. Pick me up.'"

"Yes, you could," Nora said.

"No," shrieked Elisa. "I want to pick up Airmail."

"Thanks for the offer, Nora," said Russell's mother as she and Russell and Elisa got off the elevator on the second floor. Nora and Teddy and their mother went on up to the seventh floor.

Supper was a dismal meal. Elisa continued to

cry, and Russell felt worse and worse that he hadn't said anything about Airmail when they had left the library. He really didn't know that her stupid old doll was so important to Elisa. In the middle of supper, he jumped up from the table and got his favorite car from the bedroom. It was bright red and ran with a battery.

"You can play with my car," he offered when he returned with it to the table.

Even though Elisa often begged Russell to be allowed to play with this special car of his, she just shook her head from side to side. She didn't want to play with it now. She wanted Airmail.

Their father picked up Elisa and took her from the table. "Would you like me to read one of your library books to you?"

That was the worst thing he could have said. The word *library* reminded Elisa where Airmail was at this very moment. And she began to howl worse than ever.

"How about a nice bubble bath?" suggested Mrs. Michaels.

Elisa just kept on howling. Russell felt like

crying, too. It was a terrible thing he had done. He had known that they had left Airmail at the library, and he hadn't told them. Now Elisa was going to keep on crying all night long. Suddenly Russell thought of something.

"Elisa," he shouted over the sound of her sobbing. "Do you remember when I had my sleep-over date with Teddy? That's what Airmail is doing. Airmail is having a sleep-over date at the library."

Elisa sniffed back her tears and stopped crying.

"Airmail is having a sleep-over date at the library," she said, and almost smiled. She thought for a moment. "They don't have any beds in the library," she said.

"Dolls don't need real beds," said her mother. "They can sleep anywhere. Remember the time Airmail slept under the dining-room table?"

"I slept under the dining-room table, too," Elisa remembered.

"You sure did," said Mr. Michaels.

85

"Tomorrow when we bring Airmail home, we should have a big party," suggested Russell.

Elisa looked at her mother for confirmation. "A party for Airmail?" she asked.

"That's a wonderful plan," Mrs. Michaels said. "We could bake a cake tonight, and tomorrow we'll invite Nora and Teddy and Annie Chu and have a welcome-home party for Airmail."

"Don't forget me," said Russell.

"Of course not," said his mother. "After all, it was your idea. Elisa, you are lucky to have such a smart brother as Russell, who knows about sleep-over dates and parties."

So Elisa and Russell helped bake a chocolate cake. That was the kind of cake that Airmail liked best, according to Elisa, and everyone thought she ought to know. Instead of frosting, Elisa said she wanted her mother to sprinkle the cake with *soft sugar*. Russell smiled with superiority. He knew she meant confectioners' sugar, which was soft and powdery.

"I'll put it on tomorrow before I serve the

86

cake," Mrs. Michaels promised as the children licked out the bowl together.

Elisa almost cried again when she got into bed and Airmail wasn't there. But Russell reminded her about the doll's sleep-over date, and so she put her thumb in her mouth and didn't cry at all.

In the morning they were at the library when the door opened at ten A.M. And sure enough, sitting on the front desk was Airmail, who was waiting for them to take her home. In the afternoon, Nora and Teddy and Annie all came, and they had a welcome-home party. It was a lot of fun, and Russell decided that it wasn't so bad to have a little sister who carried a doll around with her all the time. It was much better than having her cry.

They played musical chairs and hot potato, and then they sat around the table for cake and milk. "Put a candle on the cake," Elisa said.

"Is it Airmail's birthday?" asked Nora.

"Yes," Elisa decided. "And I am going to help Airmail blow out the candle."

When the candle was placed in the center of the cake and lighted, Elisa took a deep breath and blew it out. Suddenly the air was filled with all the powdered sugar blowing off the cake. As the sugar landed on all the children, it was like a little snowstorm right on the table. It was the second best moment of the day, thought Russell. The best moment had been when Airmail was found and Elisa was smiling. Russell remembered and he smiled, too.